GOBLIN MOON

Written and illustrated by **Jacqueline Rogers**

HARPER
An Imprint of HarperCollinsPublishers

For my daughters, Martha and Emma

Goblin Moon
Copyright © 2019 by Jacqueline Rogers
All rights reserved. Manufactured in China.
No part of this book may be used or reproduced in any manner whatsoever
without written permission except in the case of brief quotations embodied in
critical articles and reviews. For information address HarperCollins Children's Books,
a division of HarperCollins Publishers, 195 Broadway, New York, NY 10007.
www.harpercollinschildrens.com

ISBN 978-0-06-279229-7

The artist used gouache on Fabriano Artistico paper with
a digital line to create the illustrations for this book.
Typography by Rachel Zegar
19 20 21 22 23 SCP 10 9 8 7 6 5 4 3 2 1
❖
First Edition

Old Goblin Moon,
rising up soon . . .
peeks through the trees,
picks up the breeze,

sets leaves to dancing
as day drifts to night,
outshines the stars
with its glowing blue light.

The Goblin Moon beams
in its own eerie way,
casting strange shadows
that frolic and sway.

Better get home now
and snug up inside.

The goblins are coming—
we better go hide!

The moon calls them out.
I think I can hear
the rustling and chattering
as they get near.

They dance and they swoon,
they whoop and they play.

They see me up here!
Then scatter away. . . .

But where did they go?
Are they done having fun?

Hey, what's that noise?
I just saw something run!

What's in the corner?

Who's under the bed?

What scurried by me?

Who crumbled the bread?

"Go **BACK** to your **MOON!**
You're scaring the baby!"

But why won't they leave?

Well, now what?

Hmmm . . . maybe . . .

they need something special,
some Halloween treats?
They'll leave if they're given
a long trail of sweets!

Back to your goblin-y
fathers and mothers.
Go join the moon dance—
here's treats for the others.

Old Goblin Moon
finally drifts down,
and sleepy goblins head home
to their dens underground.

"Well, Goblin Moon,
GOOD NIGHT TO YOU!"
Another Halloween gone,
and my candy, too!

Finally to bed.
A knock?

I'll go see. . . .

A goblin-y treat made special FOR ME!